THE RIVERS RUN DEEP

2019

An Anthology of short stories
from the Northern Rivers
region of
New South Wales.

Proudly presented by the
Australasian Order of Old Bastards

THE RIVERS RUN DEEP 2019
*Anthology Copyright © 2019 Australasian Order
of Old Bastards, Northern Rivers Branch
Individual story copyright is retained by
the individual authors.
All rights reserved.*

ISBN: 978-0-9946174-7-7

*Published by **Meredian Pictures & Words** 2019
Ballina, Australia*

MEREDIAN
PICTURES & WORDS

INSPIRING IMAGINATION

Table of Contents

THE DINGO

By BETTE GUY

Bette Guy has won numerous awards as an author and play-wright, including the Patrick White Playwright's Award.

Since coming to Australia from England, Bette has immersed herself in many aspects of her adopted country – travelling and talking to people. This story shows how much she's learned about, and how much regard she has for, those living on the land. She may not live in the harsh part of "the bush", but she certainly understands it.

It was another hot summer's day, the third year of a drought. Eva Jackson had not seen such a dry year since the big one in nineteen sixty-four. She and David had worked hard to keep the place going but after he got back from Vietnam he lost interest. It was the nightmares that tipped him over the edge, gnawing away at him like a dog with a bone, too hard to swallow, too big to bury. The death certificate stated heart failure. Failure of the mind more like, a mind broken by the war. He'd tried to mend himself with his own array of drugs but the overdose finally finished him off in eighty-one. She'd been alone since then, they'd somehow never got round to having kids. Good job, she used to tell herself, conscription just might come back.

Their station was classified as a good sheep block but now and then the country, knowing better, paid white fellas back for their bad judgement. Every day more sheep were dying. No need of shearers this year. Nothing but future dingo meals roamed the paddocks. There was not a skerrick of decent fodder left on the place, even the last scraps of wilga had been eaten up. No cash left to buy feed, dams near enough empty and the one remaining bore pumping out less and less. Eva could only just afford a few pellets to keep Sally, the milker, producing. She fed herself on scraggy carcasses. She'd worked the place for over twenty years on her own, living like a man, thinking like a man, doing the work of a man but it seemed neither man nor woman would beat this drought.

In town they'd told her about the government packages; short term grants, long term loans, financial and agricultural advisers. They all required bundles of paperwork and excessive prying into a person's personal affairs. Not that there was much personal stuff to pry into and she'd certainly had no affairs since that fling with the shearers cook way back in eighty-six. Anyway, her family had always been a proud mob, disapproving of both bureaucracy and charity. The farm was a way of life for her, not a business. Same as it was for her father, until the bankruptcy, wool fetching next to nothing and the banks wanting their money. Eva pulled expertly at Sally's teats.

"When exactly was that, old girl? Seems like a lifetime ago."

It almost was. Sixty years in fact. She was a little kid then, running around with the black fellas who camped down by the creek on what they said was their land. Back then no white people ever questioned that belief. White people owned the freehold or held perpetual leases - that was all that mattered to people like her father and the others. But then it was 'pay up or bail out', from the bank. While her father had been happy to give work to the aborigines when it was his own place he couldn't let them back on the place once the bank took it off him. He'd stayed on as Manager and couldn't face the humiliation of them seeing him working for a master, same as they'd done for him. He'd told his daughter a thousand times.

"I sold out as well as sold up."

He'd gone to his grave a bitter man. Years later, when times were good and wool prices rocketed, she and David took on a mortgage and bought the place back. They were doing real well. Then he was conscripted. Vietnam changed things forever. David's nightmares, his death, her left to see it all through. And now another bad drought, perhaps enough to finish her off.

No matter what the forecast, every morning, Eva Jackson strode out into the home paddock, scouring the skies for signs of rain. When there was none she'd mooch back into the house and after a strong cup of tea quickly slurped down, she'd fill the water bag, shove a red and white cotton scarf into her pants and grab her rifle and ammunition. Then she'd saddle up Rudi and ride out to check on the numbers of sheep that hadn't survived the night. The dead ones were roped up and with Rudi taking most of the weight, they were dragged to a pile, where they were burnt, the stench filtering through the scarf mask to her quivering nostrils. Some, so close to death it didn't matter, she killed.

A dingo had lately taken to following her into the far paddocks, trotting a short distance behind. Neither one of them had reason to fear the other. She'd grown up with dingos about the place, and there was plenty of meat on offer for the animal. Once, Rudi kicked out at it but after neatly avoiding the hoof, the dingo returned to exactly the same spot. She'd called out to it from her perch in the saddle.

"You're either a very brave dingo or a very stupid one!"

 The dingo continued behind the mounted horse. This scenario had occurred every day for months now. As the country became drier sheep numbers dwindled. Rudi grew thinner, the district dingos grew fatter. Eva Jackson's shirts and moleskins became baggy on her wiry body. Luxuries like chocolate cake and pavlova were no longer baked, she was down to basics. With the best of intentions the well stocked store at Winterton had kindly offered her credit, but she'd politely refused. The well fed dingo that accompanied her gained both weight and resolution, never missing a chance to join her on the daily rounds.

 She'd told herself plenty of times that

she'd be better walking off the place. She could find some kind of work in the city. The surviving flock would simply have to die without her. Each day they grew more restless as they roamed the dusty ochre earth in search of a few dried up stalks. Recklessly perhaps, she stayed on, praying earnestly for rain, even though she'd given up on God the year her husband died. Drastic times call for drastic measures.

During the days the solitary dingo padded beside her as she travelled the property checking on the death count. In the evenings, swaying in her father's old rocker on the verandah, she'd eye the dingo sitting courteously a few paces away. In a sense it replaced the working dogs, which she'd had to kill when they finished off the last of her chooks. She was an experienced shot, the dogs had no time to even whimper before they fell. At the time she'd felt tempted to shoot a couple of the dingos around the place, although she had absolutely no reason to. In normal seasons she'd only lose a dozen or so lambs to them. If humans provided such readily accessible meals why would the dingos refuse the opportunity?

As they sat apart one evening, Eva pondered on how smart the dingo is, as a species. It was a clear night, the brilliant sunset dangling over the distant creek bed, the haze of dry heat and dust diffusing the fire-glow scene into a rose-hued impressionist picture. She accepted how it was Nature's prerogative to provide both wonder and pain in more or less equal amounts.

*

It was the morning she finally decided to walk off the place that the accident happened. It was the photograph of David that was the root cause. Eva's routine was to kiss David's image each night before getting into bed and, each morning, to throw the same photo a kiss as she hurried across the creaking timber floor to the bathroom down the hall. This morning had been different.

She'd woken in the middle of a nightmare in which her father was dragging her off the farm. She was hog tied, just like the dead sheep she and Rudi dragged to the funeral pyre. Her father was going to burn her alive! In the terror of the dream her flailing arms knocked the photograph off the bedside table. The sound of breaking glass woke her.

There it was, laying on the pink and green floral rug, the glass a thousand shards, David's face staring up at her, his smile wistful. It took her ages to clear up the mess but even longer for her mind to return to anything like its calm self. The photograph she placed under her pillow for safe keeping.

After her usual cup of tea she began the daily ritual of riding the paddocks. She was still distracted by the nightmare and failed to concentrate as she usually did on guiding a half starved Rudi down towards the dried out creek bed. Weakness caused the horse to lose its footing and he stumbled over twisted roots, throwing his mistress against the trunk of a brigalow. She heard the thud as her head made contact, then it all went black.

When she came to, the position of the sun told her it was late afternoon. She never wore a watch. Her throat rasped as she tried to call out. Her stomach grumbled violently. She suspected she'd been unconscious overnight. Her thigh bone was sticking right out through the skin, blood congealing around the wound and flies buzzing. Her shoulder and right arm were a painful mess. There was no sign of Rudi but there were plenty signs of dingoes. A pack was carefully circling her, their feet plodding on the compacted earth, their curiosity drawing them closer to her.

She inched herself up into a sitting position, leaning the undamaged half of her body against the tree that had knocked her out. Already ants were trekking up and down her damaged thigh, devouring little bits of blood, dead skin and oozing gunk. The flies awaited the appropriate time to regenerate their own kind on her dead body. She did her best to stem the blood with the scarf.

Her eyes scoured the ground for the rifle. It was just beyond her reach. She would have to crawl to retrieve it. She made several attempts but failed, the pain overwhelming her. Her head began to thump. The rest of her body was numb. Her dingo appeared and growled a thick message to the pack which, reluctantly, dispersed. She mumbled hoarsely to it.

"Want me all to yourself, do you fella? Well, I won't go without a fight."

 She was pointing at the rifle as she spoke. The dingo stared first at the rifle, then at Eva Jackson. It trotted over to the weapon, grabbed the butt end and dragged it within her reach. It backed off, waiting. Eva stared in awe, reasoning that the dog must once have been part of an Aboriginal Camp and had learnt the trick.

 She placed her left hand on the rifle, its familiar smoothness a comfort to her increasingly frightened state. She settled back staring up at the cloudless sky, the brightness of its blue hurting her eyes.

Soon there would be little shelter from the heat, in spite of the leaved branches stretching out above her. She badly needed water. Her water bag had disappeared with Rudi. She scratched at the soil, found and put a small piece of stone in her mouth and sucked. It bought sufficient saliva for temporary relief. She called out Rudi's name, over and over. There was no whinnying response, no rustling of horse flesh against dehydrated bush, no friendly ambling of hooves towards her. She picked up the rifle and checked her pockets for ammunition. She spoke to the dingo again.

"So, you trust me not to shoot you, which I could, easy. But I won't. Not yet anyhow."

The dingo did not move. Eva Jackson's vision began to blur as she faded into darkness. When she awoke the stars twinkled with the enthusiasm of the uninvolved, reminding her of when she was a kid sleeping out on the verandah of the main house. She felt for the rifle. It was still there.

Her hand slipped off the weapon onto a damp, solid lump. For a second she thought it must be her wounded leg she was touching but drawing her hand carefully over the strange shape she realised it was a piece of meat, torn from a freshly dead sheep. A gift of life. Her eyes searched for her saviour, for the person who'd come to her rescue. She saw no one. She sucked long and hard on the tough meat, then, tearing off a small piece, she chewed, extremely slowly. She'd had liquid and food, now all she had to do was to get herself out of there.

She summed up her options. In her condition she'd be unlikely to survive crawling the five kilometres back to the homestead. Sooner or later she'd die from dehydration, or blood loss, or both. There were four rounds in the rifle. She had to keep one back for herself, just in case. If she shot three rapid rounds into the air she wondered, would someone recognise it as a distress signal? An SOS? Her closest neighbours were forty kilometres one way and just under twenty the other. How far would the sound resonate? It was her best chance, perhaps her only chance. Without further enquiry into the sense of the action she loaded and fired off three rounds in rapid succession and lay back, drained of every emotion. The dingo trotted over to her and, keeping his distance, stood guard.

"Thanks for saving my life, old fella. Let's hope the neighbours are as smart as you are."

She reached out her good arm to try to

pat the dingo. She wanted the dingo to know she was grateful for what it had done but it settled down beyond her reach.

*

The moon was waning when headlights beamed eerily in the distance, like two close points of a compass, cutting through the dark unmarked space between day and night, between life and death. Eva let off the final round as a marker. As soon as the truck was close the dingo padded stealthily away, vanishing into its unknowable world.

The neighbours took Eva to the base hospital, some hundred kilometres away. No use waiting for a helicopter, they'd decided. They secured her body best as they could to make her comfortable for the long journey. The truck lurched and bumped over the corrugated roads trailing a cloud of fine dust behind it, until reaching the smooth black security of the bitumen. Eva's thoughts turned to David and she sobbed quietly to herself.

The patient was soon fixed up. In time the bones would heal. However, because of her age, she was to be kept under observation for a while.

A week later the radio announcer ecstatically declared the breaking of the drought. Steady rain running down the hospital windows triumphantly confirmed the news. Sitting up in bed, crisp white sheets tucked up under her arms, Eva thought about the farm and how the dams would be filling up. Soon vegetation would return providing some feed for the remaining flock. She thought about Sally and Rudi who'd been caught and kept alive by neighbours.

She imagined the dingos frolicking in the wet, their joyous splashing in the creek, their dashing up and down, the shaking of their bodies, the absolute joy of life embedded in their genetic makeup. No doubt the black fellas were doing exactly the same thing, each at one with their unpredictable country.

She thought of David's photograph tucked under her pillow. When she was better she'd find herself that job in the city and spend weekends at the farm and maybe, once conditions got really good again, she'd go back there to live fulltime. David would want her to keep on trying. She hoped her dingo would wait for her.

.o0o.

NINE CONCUBINES

By KARL JOHNSTON

A student of so many different disciplines that he wryly describes himself as "probably over-qualified for jobs that haven't been invented yet", Karl Johnston is a writer fascinated by how things work.

That fascination extends to people, and relationships. This story has some of the style and overtones of the Arabian Nights and Arthurian legend, and more than a touch of whimsy, as it delves into the mind of a powerful but lonely man.

The Emperor donned his armour of sapphire steel, livery of turquoise and blood-rust black, and his crown of many horns. He took up his blade Kingsever. Gathered he his Surgeon-Generals atop six squealing mounts.   They rode.

The emperor's first concubine arose. She breakfasted in private, a platter of fruits and pastries having been placed in the antechamber. Then she attended to her personal bathe in the high-walled water feature, all crystal and effervescence. Next she played practice a while upon the flute, and a wondrous keening was heard throughout the vicinity. "The Lady is well familiar with her Arts!" the staff did tell, for the first concubine's abilities were highly regarded throughout the court and all the land.

Then she made ready herself by all the means she possessed. Her lustrous black hair she coiled tight atop her regal head, the requisite seven wisps allowed free in semblance of immodesty. Her nails, hand and foot, she trimmed and painted pink, for not even the symbol of an unsheathed blade was permitted in the presence of the Emperor in his citadel. Her exquisite pale flesh she anointed with his preferred fragrant essence. Her single robe, precariously bound with fragile buttons and frail wisps, she affixed to her lithe form.

Finally her pretty face she painted thick with pure white, her eyes a fierce crimson: a newly born visage, unseen by any man alive.

Returned she to her circular bedding to lay. White ribbon she bound her eyes with, unless to catch any glimpse of her Master the Emperor upon his return. And there she did await his pleasure, and await.

The Emperor, his Generals, their staff and the Army of the Realm took war to the Caliphate, the despised enemy. And victory glorious they brought back to the citadel in the city.

All hailed the Emperor for his wisdom and ruthlessness, his might and holiness. All praised their great fortune in being advanced one step closer to heavenly perfection. The Emperor blessed them each and every, an accomplishment achieved with the merest flick of his wrist. And then retired to his quarter.

He doffed his regalia, and bathed. A mighty sigh was heard around the vicinity. "Our Lord doth recover his strength, against all his majestic feats to come!" the staff did tell each other. The apothecary tended him of some minor abrasions and an uncomfortable chafe, whereupon the horse master was roundly whipped and garroted.

Then did the Emperor visit upon his first concubine, so to take well-earned and rightful refreshment. It must be assumed he did lay with her and engage in blissful congress, and that they did anoint each one the other with the fruits of their love's labours, for what other should a man of stature require of a woman of elevated position. (If mere man he truly be, for upon this we shall not speculate.)

It must be assumed because no eyes spied upon them that night nor any other, upon pain of blinding, castrating and beheading. It was observed and verified, however, that the Emperor did depart the bedchamber much later, and in especially high spirits, and wearing a regal sheen upon his proud, limpid person.

But he never saw her face.

The next day dawned, as it so often does and evermore shall. The Emperor donned his ceremonial robes and the comfy coronet, the one with the extra padding behind the ears, and the silken slippers cunningly crafted to resemble steel with rivets.

This day was taxation review day, and the Emperor was required to adjudicate upon disputes, to endorse the annual takings, and to decree the coming year's legislations. He would have preferred the dungeon master to settle the disputes and the treasurer the rest, but tradition was tradition, so what can one do? He quietly directed the citadel concierge to light an extra censer of special recipe nearby, and submerged himself in the funk of proceedings.

The Emperor's second concubine arose. She arose late and spent much of the day in playful pursuit, because she was full aware of the length and density of taxation day, and of the extent of the Emperor's regard for the day's worth in the great scheme of things, and of the length and density of the citadel concierge's special herbage. Thus she conserved her strengths, bathed late, and made herself prepared at an appropriate hour.

In white face and white mask, and upon her white bed, she awaited.

At the end of the hour of supplication after the hours of deliberations, the Emperor burst into the bedding chamber in a rage and vented a fearsome roar. She the second concubine quailed within herself. Then the Emperor observed her comely curves displayed before him and his anger cooled or was otherwise diverted. His masculine fires burned then all the hotter, and their union was both forged and quenched. All this is again surmised.

He never saw her face.

Early upon the next day, the Emperor was

roused from his slumber by the sounds of commotion most violent, from proximity unacceptable. Eschewing the protective padded greatcoat proffered by his valets, he took up a stoking iron and strode forth in his lavender night dress, towards the affray.

His personal guards were beset by a gang of rebel ruffians in the storeroom adjoining the pantry masters' stations. Evidently they had ascended via the bucket and chain from the underground spring and were bent on assassination most foul.

The Emperor joined battle on his own behalf. With utmost force and precision, he broke limbs, pierced eyes, and subjugated the stragglers. Several of the scoundrels lay dead, but others survived until the end of that day.

In the meantime, the third concubine was

awoken by way of messenger ostrich, ungainly but reliable. (The ostrich, not the concubine.) Whilst the Emperor engaged in interrogation, she raised her hair with hurry, covered her face, and alit the bed. She was still tying the silk when he strode in, all roused by the precision of the new Inquisitor's techniques.

For the Emperor to arrive at such an early hour of the morn, with such shortness of notice, was a serious breach of the covenant between Master and third, or practically any other, concubine. Equally in breach was the lady herself, clad as she was in a common (though comfortable, and noticeably slight) nightie. Their mutual transgressions must surely have magnified whatever other intrusions occupied them that morn, it is believed.

The Emperor was observed to sleep long and deep, after, and a sonorous snore re verberated throughout the vicinity, rapidly vacated out of respect.

And he never saw her face.

The court and the populace had long anticipated the following day with electrical excitement. The Anniversary of the Emperor's descent to the Realm had arrived. No amount of celebration would be too small or too extravagant upon such an occasion. One recalls the moat set on fire last year, and the impromptu feast of piglets the year before.

The Emperor allowed himself to be conducted to a few of the more dignified festivities, and thereafter attended some carousing whilst disguised as a prosperous beggar and supplicant. He soon tired though of the maintenance of required jollity, and returned through secret passage to his quarter.

The fourth concubine had anticipated the Emperor's weariness. She presented a light repast of tasty, nutritious and extravagant morsels, and a healthy supply of dark and light ales, meads and ciders. Thusly heartened, they took to her bed for some cuddles, some spooning, and some come what may. Probably.

But he never saw her face.

At the next day, a foreign dignitary arrived with slightest fanfare or forewarning. A day early. The Emperor felt not like seeing her nor anybody else. So he didn't see her face at all, not even the makeup. She was the fifth concubine.

The next was the day of a great and grand wedding. He had forgotten about it, and with himself debated whether to attend. Eventually though his protocol masters and the jester convinced him. Swiftly he dressed, and slowly he remembered to dispatch a courier to purchase a few gifts from the citadel souvenir shop, and arrived in time to observe the vows.

It was his first concubine, now released and free to marry that businessman who was always mooching around the court. Probably never get rid of him now. Must remember to add his name to the dungeon master's to-do list.

He saw then her face! Pretty. She must always have been so pretty. And the sixth concubine received a right and royal bollocking that night, a treatment she failed to appreciate and she told him so. Most emphatically. The whole vicinity and several other nearby vicinities heard that argument. He certainly did not see her face, but he almost saw the back of her hand. Allegedly.

The next day the fountains stopped working and the high-walled water feature flooded and the springwater chain broke and a ghastly stench emanated from the meat safe of nearby. Then the master plumbers took an age to arrive and they brought the wrong tools, at which time new plumbers who were still alive had to be fetched from the villages.

None of the Dukes or Generals knew anything about plumbing, softy southerners, so the Emperor had to supervise.

The flooding ruined the seventh concubine's entire wardrobe, shoes too, so she had to borrow a handmaiden's finest clothes, which were not very fine at all.

The makeup was dry, at least she got that bit working right. But when she made to don the white blindfold, it was sodden and a bit rank. O what was she to do?

And so it was that the unwashed Emperor stalked into the bedchamber and annex and saw her. He saw her white clad face, for it was unbound, and she saw his. Twas but a glimpse, but the deed was done.

She gasped and cowered, and averted her eyes, and fully expected to become flame-consumed or dungeon foddered, or struck amighty. But the Emperor spied a suspicion of her handsomeness and saw also her abject reverence for him, and he took pity upon her. His pity took the form of loving respect, as though between equals or partners. He bade her to look upon him, not as an Emperor but as a man. And so the seventh concubine did.

He knew passion that night. And he nearly saw her face. He did see her soul, and she his. But the covenant between Master and concubine forbade attachments, even little quick ones. So it was that they parted in the morning. Yet part of each of them both remained conjoined.

In the hour before the dawn of the following day, sentries reported a strange new light on the sky horizon. A point of white, trailing a long mist. Master viziers bade the Emperor be summoned. Studied he that light until the sun itself rose beneath it. Conferring with the aged masters of astronomics and astrologistics, he announced the need for a pondering.

He pondered long and he pondered deep, and at the midmorn he awoke from a particularly deep and refreshing ponder, keen and alert. After quick reference with the master of portents, the Emperor made a speech which concluded that bounty and security and good health was assured for all.

This quelled any murmurings among

the peoples, and the rest of the day was consumed in the giving of thanks through the taking of libation. To provide further reassurance, the Emperor mingled himself into their midsts. He did not hide in any disguise, but rather he mingled freely, attending their ceremonies, speaking encouraging words, and partaking a little of their offerings. But it was soon noted that the Emperor seemed a little distracted, a little reserved.

Unbeknownst to any, the Emperor came to perceive that none of these faces were her angelic white face of the night before, none of the voices were as melodious, and none of these people present could claim his attentions as she did even in her absence.

When able, he took to the rooms of the eighth concubine, intending to purge this unbecoming wistfulness. Well trained, she was, and most skilled with hand and voice, and body. Though unsighted, she plied her full Art. This pleased the Emperor adequately but not mightily, for he remained distracted. It was remarked within the court that he ambled to his chambers as though unwell.

And he did not see her face. He saw another face instead.

The following was a day of distractions. The sudden and mostly unexpected death of a minor courtier required investigation, and an investigation into the investigation. The portent in the sky had brightened and needed another ponder or two. The plumbings functioned erratically. The body of a businessman could not be dispatched without a royal seal upon its forehead. The new cider vintage had been delivered and required appraisal. It was too bitter. It was all too bitter.

It was as the ninth concubine commenced her personal preparations that the Emperor decided. "Fetch unto me my sixth and seventh concubines!"

This decree caused much consternation and a flurry, a veritable storm of activity, most of it vocal. Such a demand had never been made. However, it soon happened that the sixth was the first to make ready and arrive.

"You do displease me mightily." She hung her head in consternation. How had she failed? "I have admiration for your spirit-edness. I do. Yet such a one can have no place in my harem."

She attempted a protest that only inflamed him the more.

He took up Kingsever and dispatched the Lady with a thrust and a twist. "There shall be a new propriety in my quarter."

The deed was done. He cleaned the blade
and replaced it above the mantel. Then
the ninth concubine, the senior of all the
Ladies, entered, six others behind her.
"Master. Might I be permitted to speak?"
She had removed her blindfold, though
she did affix her sight to the body on the
blooded carpet.

The Emperor felt by turns exhausted,
and ashamed, and intrigued, and (truth
be told) by a small measure, aroused. He
faced these women, and acceded.

"Majesty. Upon the wedding of the first
concubine, we numbered eight. Now your
Majesty has slain the seventh, I regret."
The blindfolded heads were lowered.
"Must also we await our executions?"

But the Emperor did then produce a sob

and a wail that broke open the hearts of all that heard, just as his own was broke.

"What have I...?" He had slain the one who broached his defenses, and slew his reserve, and invaded the heart he once, only once, possessed. Such a love would never again be his, he knew.

"Majesty. We await our doom."

But he relented. That love had fled him. But he had seen it, its face. He knew it lived somewhere in the land, or even the citadel itself. And that love should be had, if not by himself, then by someone. Or all. Such love was a vital and valuable thing. And if it were possible, he would set this realm to nurturing it. A new crop, and a new currency for his land.

He commanded, though gently, "Wash her face."

This was done. He gazed upon her face, for the first time and the last.

Then he regarded his concubines that remained. "Which of you was my sixth, previously?"

That one shrank back for a moment, but gathered herself and stepped forward. The senior Lady brought her to the fore.

"I will not slay you, nor any other. There has been too much wrongful death in my name. Any name." He let fall a single tear. "Remove your blinds. All of you."

And they all saw each the other, and all wept a little.

In time the Emperor wedded himself to his Lady, the former sixth concubine, the one with the feisty spirit. The other Ladies he did free, though did not abandon.

They remained as senior courtiers and counselors, ones with more insight and wisdom than most, adept as they were in the ways of men and women, kings and peoples. And the realm did prosper.

For the rest of their days the Emperor and the Empress lived as equals in their differences. They played well and ruled well, his compassion tempered by her firm intellect. And they awoke each morning the way they slept each night, always face to face.

.o0o.

HER NAME WAS UHIB

By STEVE NOSSITER

It takes a special sort of writer to convincingly take us into a non-human mind. Steve Nossiter has a passion for it. His stories don't 'humanise' plants and animals – they seek to find their subject's own perspective.

Uhib is a loose translation of an Arabic word meaning 'loved'. Her mother's name – Hubb – is a similarly sourced word for 'love'. Both are appropriate. This is a story of a love and a life that runs deep into the Earth.

Her name was Uhib, although at this point she wasn't aware of that. She wasn't even aware she had a name at all. She was awake, alive, senses just starting to fire, a growing realization of being and an absolute feeling of awe.

Overwhelming and encapsulating all of this was a single idea, the most important thing in her world. This one idea was, Grow.

And so Uhib grew, pushing upwards through darkness and dirt and in a moment of wonder and relief, she discovered the sun, warm on her bright green stalk. She lay her old home, her empty seed husk, gently on the soil beside her as she turned her gaze towards the sky and, filled with light and warmth from the morning light, she continued her skyward climb.

And as she rose higher, downwards she also reached, each millimeter introducing a new and refreshing sensation of satisfaction, quenching her insatiable thirst as her soft, new roots began drinking in the moisture and nutrients from Earth. Immediately Uhib pulled the cool liquid up into her stalk and into her new, pointy green leaves and felt a gentle tingle as the water disappeared and a new, sweet liquid began its syrupy journey back down her stalk giving her strength and giving back to Earth below.

As time passed, Uhib became strong. Her stem became brown and firm, which she was glad about after a few windy days made her leaves rub against her young green stem. She had a lot of little branches now and some down low that she was really proud of. They were covered in leaves and almost as thick as her trunk. Up the top she kept making new thin branches and lovely little new leaves were appearing every day. Uhib loved to imagine what her branches might look like one day.

There were lots of trees around Uhib but one in particular took her imagination to places the other trees didn't. It was so tall, so wide and sometimes she felt a little tingle when one of Uhib's tiny roots brushed up against its enormous ones. She often wondered how far into the forest these roots stretched and could only imagine how much Earth and air her giant friend was connected with. She wondered how much it knew, how much it had experienced and she wondered if she would ever grow to be so majestic.

She loved the little ants and bugs that climbed all over her leaves each day, and learned to tolerate the creepy worms and things that rubbed against her roots. But one of Uhib's favourite things to do every morning was to wait for the funny little birds, the Noisy Miners to wake up.

She was really relaxed at this time of day. The sun hadn't quite begun its journey over the sky and so it wasn't time to start growing again yet. The Earth was cool and the air was usually so still. As the grey light swelled over the tall trees and the kookaburras started making a racket way over at the edge of the forest some-where, she waited for the first movement.

It wasn't in her branches yet. She was still too small even for little birds to land there, but they roosted every night on a bigger tree just near her. It would start with one of them, slowly untucking its head from under its wing, looking around for a bit then doing a couple of tired little chirps.

Before long a whole flock of them were flitting around and singing out to each other across all the trees. Uhib couldn't understand what they said but they seemed to all be mostly saying the same thing to each other. Maybe they were just saying 'Good morning', or 'Where are we going today?' but Uhib liked to imagine that they were saying something more like 'Look at Uhib. She's grown so much and is becoming such a pretty tree.' She was probably right too, because now she was no longer a plant but a beautiful, thriving young tree.

One morning she didn't hear the miners, on account of the rain. Uhib loved rain. It made her roots feel so cool and nice, gave her leaves a lovely massage and gave her plenty to drink. It was lovely, especially after hot days. The noisy miners didn't really seem too affected by the rain most times but this was a lot of rain and so the miners must have been huddled a bit further into the forest under some bigger branches.

'Oh well', she thought. 'They'll come back later when the rain stops.'

But later on, the rain didn't stop. It didn't even stop and start again like it sometimes does on the really rainy days It just kept falling, and falling. And it was heavy. Uhib wondered where all the rain came from. It was like a whole world up there just broke open and is spilling down onto this world.

'That's ok,' thought Uhib. 'I can't seem to get enough water lately.' But soon Uhib had taken in plenty of water and was starting to feel very heavy and tired.

Night fell and the dark grey faded into an even darker grey, and still the rain thundered down. Uhib slept.

When the morning came, the grey hue started to reveal something Uhib hadn't seen before. She felt a tingling in her roots adjacent to the big tree again and smelled something urgent and alarming through her leaves. On the ground all around Uhib was water and it was flowing fast.

'That wasn't there yesterday,' Uhib thought, and felt a sudden surge of panic as she noticed the water wasn't just flowing past her trunk, it was wetting her roots as well. Some of the roots that were closer to the bottom of the hill were already completely surrounded by water and the soil that normally was there, her one source of food, had disappeared altogether.

The wet sky grew brighter as Uhib felt the water removing more and more soil from her roots.

'Oh, no.' she thought. 'This is not supposed to happen. Why is this happening?'

She fought against increasing surges of muddy water now making its way up her trunk and engulfing her lower branches.

'I just need to hold on. Let me hold on.'

She felt another tingle in her roots as another small tree smashed past her breaking off one of her proud limbs. 'Sun, where are you? Please!' she cried.

Another branch was grappled so hard by the raging flood it broke on one side and was left limply flicking about under the surface of the debris and water. Uhib felt for a stone that she'd wrapped her roots around when she was young and was shocked to feel it start to move in the current. The soil had eroded completely from it's lower side and was now threatening to let it go altogether.

She felt another tingle from the big tree

root, and perhaps she would have been strengthened by this small connection, but Uhib was no longer thinking about her giant friend. Her roots and trunk were almost completely surrounded by water now. She could no longer hold herself upright. Reaching for the sky, listening to the chirp of happy birds, growing old, resilient and wise like the big tree seemed futile, now. Like a lost dream. Her leaves, only the strong ones left now, were flapping manically in the floodwater, her branches bent and broken were strained against the current and the only things left holding her here, holding her to Earth were the last few roots wrapped around the stone in what was now the bank of a flooded stream.

Uhib felt her roots, the last little sensation of soil tingling strongly now like an electric pulse and in that moment felt something in her heart like 'Release now', and she knew the only thing to do now was to let go. It was finished.

A wash of brown water finally forced its way around the stone, taking with it the last few fragments of soil that were holding it there.

Tingle. 'Release now, little one.' Uhib felt one last sway as her trunk tilted over, bringing her topmost branches into the swirling dark current, and the water, holding her fast tore Uhib from the Earth.

The rain continued into the afternoon and after a while, satisfied with its destruction, it stopped. Through the night the water receded and left behind a deep wound through the heart of the forest floor. Lines of dirt and leaves outlined the edges of the flood.

Pulse.

Uhib woke.

Pulse ... tingle.

Uhib felt her roots. Pain. Loss. Tingle.

She felt her branches. Fracture, loss, pain.

'Where am I?'

Pulse ... 'You are here little one. I have
you. You are safe now.'

As Uhib slowly woke she felt small sensa-
tions gradually beginning to come back to
her. She felt around her strange surround-
ings. Some soil, not much but she felt
relieved to feel some of her roots covered
over. With the very little strength she had,
she clung in. She was still holding in the
tangle of her tiny roots the small stone that
kept her grounded for so long. Curving
deep beneath and on either side of her
were roots. Strong thick roots. Uhib's thin
trunk was laying bent over a part of these
same roots that showed above the surface.
The bark was rough, yet comforting.

There was wet soil half covering Uhib's own thin, broken roots and part of her trunk. Her branches, partly broken and limp were draped over the large roots and on the ground around her.

Uhib felt warm light touch one of her leaves, then another, and then soon all of her leaves were being washed under the gentle warmth of sunlight. But was still too weak to take much of this in and in no shape to grow. But she was grateful for this comfort.

'Uhib, do you know where you are? Can you feel around you?' Uhib felt the familiar tingle of the thick roots now surrounding her on one side. She felt the sun streaming and filtering through high, full branches. She noticed now the huge trunk, much closer now than before, towering up into the sky.

'You caught me?' Uhib said weakly, trying her own tingling communication.

'Yes, my dear Uhib. I caught you. I have been waiting for this day for a long time.'

Uhib tried to consider this. Maybe she was too weak, maybe she was too young, but she couldn't make any sense of this. She let her thoughts drift back to her own weak body. Pain, loss ... gratitude, hope. That hope was very weak, but it was there, like a single star in a sea of black sadness.

'Thank you,' she managed.

'Uhib, I want to tell you something. Feel around you. These roots, the ones that now cradle you, they've been growing for a long time now. They were growing long before you began your own journey. I'm quite proud of them. I shaped them in a very special way and for a very special reason. Uhib, I want you to know that those roots were made for you. I made them so I could catch you.'

Uhib, her mind heavy, struggled to understand. This great tree, the giant she had always admired and wanted to grow up to be like, had been thinking of her. How did it know her? Uhib was just a small tree, barely more than a sapling, and she was a towering, ancient beauty.

'Uhib, I know this is hard for you. It is painful and confusing, but it will only be for a time. You will start growing again. You will become strong and tall and one day hundreds of birds will roost in your branches, and the forest will shape itself around your majesty, just like it has for me, and like it did for my mother before me. For now, little one, rest. Rest and know that you are safe. I have you.'

With these words inside Uhib felt a wash of peace flow through her, and as the afternoon faded, into the night she slept.

The following days saw Uhib gain strength and start straightening again. Her trunk would always have a funny kink at the base, now, but she could still drink through it and send sugary goodies back down to her roots and to the michorizal funghi that had started sharing its water with her.

She grew new leaves and started reaching up again. Hope was once again rising in her heart. She was scarred and a bit broken, no longer as pretty as she was before but she grew with a new joy and purpose.

The big tree taught her many things. She told her of how she was once small like Uhib many years ago and how her journey upwards took her through many hardships, floods, worse even than the one Uhib had just been through, droughts, beetles and other bugs boring into her branches and trunk.

She showed Uhib where huge branches had

broken off in different storms and showed
her cute little fresh shoots emerging from
her canopy.

She also told Uhib of a time when she grew
more than a million little seeds, but even
as the little seed pods were still developing
and the seeds inside hadn't fully formed yet
she chose only one. And how as the pods
opened into wooden stars and all the other
seeds spiralled away on the wind, she carefully placed this one seed on the richest soil,
and watched Uhib emerge into the sunlight.

She explained how she knew the flood
would come, as it happens frequently
through here, but that she'd designed her
root system long ago to catch Uhib and to
catch a lot of the good soil along with her.
To give her heir a strong and rich founda-
tion.

Uhib grew to know the big tree, her mother,

as Hubb. And over time she grew up, out and down, the two trees becoming strong, standing together, the great sentinels of the forest.

After many years, Hubb grew quiet, her enormous influence and majesty through the forest gradually giving way to Uhib and her own new greatness. Gradually, starting from the canopy and making her way down, Hubb stopped the flow of water to her drying leaves, letting them fall to the forest floor. In time, the tingling and pulsing communication Uhib was so accustomed to between her and her mother's roots ceased altogether. All that was left was her trunk and branches, the paling memory of a great and loving tree.

Uhib felt around her. Loss, pain ... gratitude ... love.

Her mother had left her. Uhib had now

taken her place as the great tree. But she was deeply grieving. The sadness emanating through the respecting forest around her, sharing a deep understanding and acceptance. And as she dwelt on the love of her mother, and the mother she had before her, Uhib felt a new desire stirring deep within.

She stretched her wide branches and began. Soon thousands of small drip like pods started forming, and began opening into little wooden stars. Uhib focussed her attention on one small pod, and inside that pod, among a collection of tiny wing shaped seeds, she found one.

'There you are.' She thought for a minute and gently said, 'Welcome my little Uhib. My little loved one. My name is Hubb. I am your mother.' And she gently let Uhib fall, spiralling slowly down to the moist forest floor.

.o0o.

TAKE ME AWAY

By HENRI RENNIE

Playwright and director Henri Rennie has been profoundly influenced by the late English author Sir Terry Pratchett, and the latter's death by what he called "the embuggerance of Alzheimers" was a deeply-felt loss.

For any creative person, losing the ability to communicate and express that creativity must surely be one of the most terrifying of prospects. And all too often, terminally ill patients are denied the right to choose the passage of the final stage of their life. In this story, a writer helps craft his own ending.

Imagine the sound of a bullfrog whispering.

That's what Lander's voice reminded the staff of, whenever he'd manage to make them hear him say, "Take me away, please..."

He didn't manage that often. Not any more.

It wasn't anything wrong with his throat that was the problem, although people hearing him lately for the first time tended to assume he was another victim of too many cigarettes.

Truth: the deep gravel voice was natural - he'd never been much of a smoker, other than a brief flirtation with a pipe in the mid-Sixties when he'd first been recognized as A Writer.

Scott William Lander. Creator of the *Morton the Lunatic* series of novels. The eponymous Morton was a teleporting hero who operated from a base on the moon, hence the 'Lunatic' tag. Scott couldn't resist a pun.

He was never quite a darling of the critics, especially in his early career. He was dismissed as a bit too populist, perhaps, at a time when science fiction was meant to be intellectual, deep and meaningful. Lander's work had seemed almost a throwback to the pulp fiction heroes of the Thirties, like Tarzan and Doc Savage.

But Scott and his hero were made of sterner stuff than the critics realised. When Armstrong and Aldrin kicked up the moon dust in '69, some thought that would end Morton's adventures. After all, anyone with a television now *knew* what the moon looked like. Nobody could really live there. NASA or the Russians would *know* if there was any sort of base there, wouldn't they?

Lander saw it as an opportunity, though. In his next book, *What The Eye Doesn't See*, he referred to how Morton used his own advanced technology to keep his base from the prying eyes of the space programs. It raised gentle questions about how trustworthy those agencies might really be, long before any conspiracy theorists proposed that the whole Apollo XI landing was an expensive hoax.

Scott had smiled in quiet delight when he read a magazine article headlined "DID 'LUNAR' LANDER GET IT RIGHT?"

That had all been a long time ago. Although his book appearances had become fewer and further between Morton had learned to overcome time as well as space. Alas, the same could not be said of his creator.

Scott Lander had fallen victim to the

creeping horro that was Alzheimer's Disease. It was insidious - slow and progressive. That had been the most distressing aspect of all for both Scott and his son William – both of them knew what was happening to the older man, and neither could do anything to prevent it.

After his diagnosis Scott had broken the news to Will, also an aspiring author, in a discussion about writing.

"Writers never retire," Scott had observed. "We go in and out of fashion, and in and out of passion with our muse, but writing isn't a job you can retire from. It's a compulsion."

"A need," said Will, nodding.

"Like a driving force," agreed his father, who then sighed deeply. "But I've realized I can't steer. Then I forgot and kept on trying. And kept on realizing, and forgetting, and realizing again. I spoke to the doctor about it, he did some tests, and now he's told me why. It's only going to get worse."

 It did. Scott reached the point where he could no longer safely take care of himself. Reluctantly William had helped him move into the Stadcor Nursing Home.

 The younger man simply didn't have the expertise to care for his father himself, and as the Home's sympathetic visiting doctor Margaret Archer had observed, "You two currently have a great, loving relationship. I'm sorry but that's not likely to survive the physical and emotional strains of your being his full-time carer."

 Stadcor had been the best option of a small range of bad choices. Scott had his own room with a window. It was at least clean and comfortable, and several of the staff were genuinely caring of their residents.

It wasn't cheap of course. These places never are. The CEO of the Home, Graeme Sparrow, was far more a businessman than a humanitarian.

Scott's time in the Home probably hadn't increased the rate of his deterioration. The Disease did that itself. William watched the decline, unable to prevent or even slow it.

William's distress was worsened when he became aware of the condition of some other dementia sufferers in Stadcor. In a room across the courtyard from his father's lay a bedbound man, a survivor of the war in Vietnam, whose dementia apparently had his mind trapped in some of the most horrific moments from his past.

The old soldier screamed. Whenever he was awake, and that was for much of the time. It seemed that the pictures in his head were worse when he closed his eyes.

Concerned for the ex-serviceman, his father, and the many other residents within earshot, William had looked for a way to ease the man's suffering. He approached the Home's resident Senior Nurse, Gwendolyn Garfield, asking if anything could be done to help and quieten him.

"That's God's way of punishing him," Ms Garfield said sternly.

After a moment of nonplussed pause William had asked, "Punishing him for what?"

"It's not our place to ask – to question God's motives."

"What if God's motive is to offer you the

chance to demonstrate your compassion?"

"If He wanted compassion shown to that man He would allow him to die."

William looked at the nurse wide-eyed. "You force feed him! You have orderlies hold him down while you medicate him! Maybe the poor bugger *would* die if you just let him! Why actively keep him alive when he clearly isn't enjoying the experience?"

Garfield sniffed. "Enjoyment has nothing to do with it. Life is sacred."

A scream echoed down the corridor from the veteran's room.

"That one doesn't sound it. Does my father have to hear it? It distresses him, certainly in his lucid moments but other times too, I think."

"Perhaps that's your father's penance," she said matter-of-factly.

William walked away before rage overcame him.

As Scott's condition continued to deteriorate, in his moments of awareness he despaired.

In one lucid spell he spoke to William. "My one joy left in life, besides you, lad, was writing. I've lost that. I know my memory fails me - day to day, hour to hour. I can't remember the last thing I wrote, who the characters are, how the story began, where it's going or how it will end. I do know there always has to be an ending."

"Dad, what are you asking?"

"They talk about dying with dignity, but

it's really about wanting to live with dignity, son. Not like that poor bastard down the hall. Take me away from a fate like that."

William bowed his head. "I don't think... it's not legal... I think the only place in the world that you can actually ask to die is Switzerland and Dad, with the best will in the world I don't think we can afford..."

The old writer patted his son's hand and said, "It's alright, Will. Just wanted you to know how I feel while I can still say it. While I still know who you are."

Scott smiled, trying to make that last comment light-hearted but his son saw the pain and recognised the truth – that even in his most disconnected moments part of Scott's mind knew what was happening to his consciousness. It knew, it hated and feared the knowledge, and it couldn't coherently communicate that hate and fear. That only fuelled the despair more.

 A meeting with the Stadcor Home's CEO did nothing to ease William's frustration. Graeme Sparrow had resolutely cited 'Duty of Care' when the younger author had tentatively tried to explore options.

"I'm not asking you or your staff to do away with him. Not even to assist in a suicide. But can't you let nature take it's own course? Let him fade away if that's what he wants? If he refuses medicine or food, respect his wishes and let him preserve his dignity."

 Sparrow shook his head with a thin show of regret.

"Our Charter makes it clear that our responsibility is to preserve life. That has to be our number one priority."

What the CEO didn't say aloud of course was his underlying thought: 'dead patients don't pay the bills – every day a bed lies empty is wasted'.

So William had bitterly watched his father's decline.

The old man's memory disintegrated. His vocabulary – essential for a writer – dried up. He could no longer remember words, or their meaning. Scott would stare blankly at an object: a vase, a radio, a bedpan – and not know what to call it.

Tears would roll down his face as the little part of his mind that *did* know flung itself against the walls of the disease that so brutally stopped him communicating.

Perhaps it was as well that his physical

condition was now such that his voice was failing him anyway. He had little more left in him than the repeated husky "Take me away" that had become the mantra of his despair.

During one visit William stood by his father's bed talking with the doctor. Margaret Archer was genuinely sympathetic, but as powerless as William.

"I really do wish I could help you *and* Scott, but my hands are tied," she explained. "Obviously I can't actively do anything to take his life – in the eyes of the law that would be murder, whatever the justification you or I made."

William gave a small derisive growl. "Laws made by politicians who think they have some moral high ground – the right to dictate someone's quality of life."

The doctor smiled sadly and said, "They have a legal high ground at least. Being elected gives them the authority to tell people what to do – even doctors, whether we agree or not."

The writer nodded in understanding as Margaret continued, "It's an ethical minefield – our oath is to 'do no harm' but I'm not one of those who interpret that to mean 'preserve life at all cost'. Unlike some of the staff here."

They both looked meaningfully in the direction of the Nurses' Station up the corridor where Gwendolyn Garfield held court.

Bitterly William said, "It's gotten to the point where that cow won't even let me in to see him if I've got so much as a sniffle. 'Protecting the residents' health' she says. I think she's worried I'll try to infect Dad with something to finish him off."

He was about to apologise to his father, but stopped when he saw the old man's blank gaze at the ceiling.

"Lights are on, but nobody's home," he said sadly.

"Don't be too sure," Margaret counseled. "Just because he can't react. Nothing coming out doesn't necessarily mean nothing's going in. Nurse Garfield isn't acting on my instructions..."

William started to protest, "Oh, I never thought you'd..."

The doctor waved his interruption away with a small smile. "I know. It's alright. What I was going to say though was that, to some extent she *is* doing her job properly. Patients like your father have a severely diminished resistance to infection. Their lungs are weak. Your sniffle quickly becomes his cold, then flu, and from there..."

She rested a gentle hand on Will's arm as she continued, "Did you know that pneumonia is called 'the old man's friend'? But you never heard me say that."

William laid his hand on hers and nodded. "Understood. But how can I get sick enough to infect him and still be allowed to visit? Especially when Garfield won't let me near him if I so much as blow my nose on my way through the front door."

Margaret shook her head. "Even if I had a suggestion to offer, you know that I couldn't do it."

"I know. But thank you." He looked down at his father. "See you tomorrow Dad.

Remember I love you."

The doctor and the son walked out of the room, a little closer together than usual.

Scott continued to stare at the ceiling, apparently oblivious to all that had been said. *Apparently*.

The following night found William sitting, as usual, beside his father's bed. He'd been there for quite a while, among other things helping with the early serving of the evening meal. At least that way the ailing writer seemed to accept a small quantity of food without the stress of being forced.

As Will watched the light outside dim he sighed softly and decided it was time he went home to make his own dinner.

He squeezed Scott's hand and said, more

from habit than expectation, "I'm off, Dad – do you want anything?"

The old man surprised him by shifting in the bed to face him.

"Take me away," was the familiar whisper, but this time there was a little glint in the sad tired eyes.

With obvious effort Scott inclined his head towards the window. His son followed his gaze and looked thoughtfully through the blinds at the gathering darkness.

Will nodded and squeezed his father's hand again as he quietly said, "Yes. Of course."

He stood, reached through the blinds and silently slid open the window. He felt the chill night air drift into the room. Then he turned and bowed his head to his father.

"I love you Dad, but you know you don't have to linger for me, don't you? I want you to be at peace."

His voice was little more than a murmur, but the ghost of a smile played across Scott's face. It remained there as the younger man left the room.

The smile was still there a while later as Scott watched the moon rise.

It was nearly ten o'clock when Nurse Garfield came in doing her 'bed check'. She scowled at the sight of the open window, and fleetingly glared at Scott as she strode past him to close the offending portal.

As she slid the pane shut she was startled by what sounded like a growl from the sick man behind her. She wheeled on him and for a moment looked like she would growl back. Instead she narrowed her eyes, stared balefully at him and stormed from the room.

She'd neglected to close the blinds.

Scott watched and smiled as *Morton the Lunatic*'s home seemed to glide up and across the sky. Silently he resolved to go with it.

Scott Lander was found dead in his bed the next morning.

William was called in. Sparrow made appropriate sympathetic comments, already considering who from the waiting list would get the bed and how soon.

Out of the CEO's earshot Gwendolyn Garfield grabbed Will's sleeve and harshly whispered, "I know what you did! I should call the police and have you arrested and charged!"

William looked at her impassively, held out both wrists as if to be handcuffed and said, "Take me away."

.o0o.

THE RIVER'S SECRETS

By RAY SPORNE

Ray is a man whose many and varied jobs have taken him all across the world over the years. The travel and experiences have been bountiful grist to the mill of his imagination, and under the name R. Addams he has produced some excellent 'whodunnits', from the gritty 'Chaloaw Stew' and its prequel 'I Am Chris!!' to the gentle Poppa Roy series.

This story brings out a softer side, giving thought to relationships and what makes them work. Nobody gets abducted or murdered. Probably...

"Shh, I told you. It's a secret," Mandy said. "And I promised not to tell, so please don't ask me again."

"But we are best friends aren't we?" I

asked. "And I thought we share every-thing."

"Um, yes we do, I guess," Mandy replied. "But this secret has nothing to do with you, or us, it's something only I know. And the people it's about I suppose. They know of course, but no-one else unless they tell them. I promised I won't. And I'm afraid to tell you. I think they might kill me, or worse."

"Wow!" I said. "Now you're really being mysterious."

We didn't talk for a few minutes and just watched the calming waters of the mighty Murray River as it slowly flowed past. Mandy and I were both sixteen. We had been swimming in the river and were re-laxing on the bank before heading home.

We weren't really boyfriend and girlfriend. Or maybe we were, but our relationship was something we never really formalized. We had just grown up and did everything together.

"I hate secrets," I said, trying to seem a bit philosophical. "Half the time it's something you knew a little bit about already and they are not really secrets. But you don't know that you know until you hear it. Do you know what I mean?"

Mandy grunted a response, which I took as her agreeing.

"And other times, once you know the secret you realize that you knowing doesn't really make any difference. It doesn't change your world. Which do you think this might be?" I persisted. "One which I might already know a bit about or one which won't really make any difference?"

Mandy didn't answer.

"You know secrets and lies are the things that usually break up friendships. And I don't want ours to break up Mandy." I put my arm around her shoulder and gave her a hug.

"Neither do I, Tom, ever. And I don't want to lie to you. It would have been so easy to tell you something vague to stop you asking questions, but I really don't want to do that."

"But you won't tell me the secret either?" I suggested.

"Not now Tom," Mandy said, looking in my eyes. "It's not my secret, honestly. If it was just about me I'd tell you. But it isn't. It's about someone else that I don't especially like, but I am scared of them in a way I can't explain. Can we leave it at that for now?"

I hugged her again. I suppose I was reassuring her or somehow telling her I understood, but of course I didn't, or didn't want to.

We walked part of the way home together then Mandy gave me a kiss on the cheek. "Will I see you tomorrow Tom?"

"Of course," I answered. "And if it's a nice day let's go swimming again, maybe a bit further along the river to that picnic place in Oddie's Creek Park. It's more private."

"That sounds good Tom, will you call me?" she said.

"I'll call you tonight and we can check with each other again in the morning, when we know what the weather is like," I suggested.

She kissed me on the cheek again and I gave her a quick hug.

"And thank you for understanding and being patient," Mandy said, then turned and walked towards her house.

I watched her. I am not sure if I loved her, or if we were ready for love. Mandy had been my best friend since Primary School and we shared everything. We enjoyed the same music, the same movies and we seemed to have the same taste in most things. I always liked her in whatever she wore and she seemed to like the way I dressed.

And we were almost always alone together and never seemed to get tired of each other's company.

So, I pondered, how did she have a secret about someone else, someone she was afraid of, without me knowing about it? Was it about someone at school? Was it about someone in her family?

As I walked home I tried to work out why it seemed important to me. Was it just because she knew something and I didn't? Or was I was concerned she was keeping something from me and I resented that? I wasn't sure, maybe both, or something else.

Dad was in the front yard trimming some of the bushes. He liked to keep them neat and usually cut them before he mowed the lawns, letting the mower throw the off-cuts from the bushes into the catcher, rather than pick them up separately.

"You look like you have the weight of the world on your shoulders, son," he said. "Are you and Mandy arguing?"

"No," I replied. "Nothing like that. We don't ever argue, and strangely we seem to agree on most things. Dad, can I talk to you about something?"

"Of course," he said. "Come into the shed and we'll open a couple of cold drinks. It's been a hot one today."

Dad's shed was his refuge, half of it was a workshop with a bench and a variety of tools and the other half was set up as a den, with comfortable chairs, a desk, refrigerator and a television mounted on the wall. It was his escape.

I took a few sips of the drink he opened for me.

"Dad, do you and Mum have secrets, from each other I mean?"

He looked at me a little strangely. "Of

course. Well, I do anyway," he said. "There are hundreds of things that I don't tell your mother, things that I think might upset her when they don't really matter, and won't change anything. Sort of white lies I guess you could call them. And I'm sure it's the same with her."

"What if Mum found out there was a secret you were refusing to tell her? Maybe about someone else, not about you two. Has that ever happened?"

"Now you're asking," he said. "Yes, it has happened, a couple of times. You may not remember but there was a time when I slept on a camp stretcher in here. We told you kids it was because I had been snoring, but it wasn't."

"What was it about, Dad?" I asked, intrigued.

"I never told her and I can't tell you," he said. "But it was someone else's secret, something about a couple of people. I was told and had a lot of calls from one of them over a period of a few weeks, so your Mum knew something was up but I had promised not to tell so I didn't."

"And she hit the roof by the sound of it," I said.

"Well, yes she did," he replied. "Even though I told her a hundred times it had nothing to do with her, or us. And that her knowing wouldn't change anything. She didn't accept that. In her mind I was cheating on her in some way because I knew something I was refusing to tell her. We humans are funny folk. And especially some women. They have to know the ins and outs of everything for some reason."

I explained briefly my issue with Mandy

and her secret.

Dad nodded. "Son, there are secrets and lies and a huge thing called trust. Albury is a large city, but still a small town in many ways. If there are secrets now they sometimes have a habit of coming out later, but not always. Often people take their secrets to the grave."

"But what if the secret is about something bad?" I asked. "Something that will change things somehow."

He looked at me and smiled. "Tom, we both know Mandy, and I believe if she thought it could hurt you, or affect your relationship in some way for that matter, she would tell you. What do you think?"

"Yes, I guess so." I admitted, after a few moments deliberating. "But I suppose I feel a little like you said Mum felt. I think our friendship is good but when she has a secret she won't share with me I can't help wondering if it is. It's an odd feeling. In one way I guess I don't want to miss out on something but in another way I think by sharing the secret she would be showing that she trusts me and, well, respects me I suppose."

"Fine," Dad said. "But by you insisting to know, are you showing that you trust and respect her? I mean it doesn't show that you respect her promise to someone else not to tell you, or that you trust her judgement, or that you believe her when she says it has nothing to do with you, or the both of you."

He had me there. Did I trust Mandy to make such a decision? Did I just believe the secret might affect us?

"Can I put something to you?" Dad asked.

"Sure, please," I replied.

"Let's suppose the secret is about two other people," he began. "Who are in a relationship that no-one else knows about, but somehow Mandy found out. Or it's about someone who has made a mistake and done something wrong, maybe something illegal, but not anything that would affect you. And again somehow Mandy was told or found out. Obviously her telling you wouldn't really make any difference, unless the couple in a relationship were people very close to you. Or if the other person who has done something illegal has done it to you or to someone you know and it will somehow end up concerning you."

I nodded my head, following his reasoning so far.

He continued. "So then, if it was one

of these and you knew the secret, what would you do with the information?" Dad asked.

I thought about it for a minute or two.

"I guess nothing. Unless I thought that one day it may end up having something to do with me," I said.

"But you don't trust Mandy to make that decision?" he replied.

He was right of course. It was my issue, my problem. Something I needed to come to terms with.

"What about Mum?" I asked, changing the subject a little. "Has she had secrets she refused to share with you?"

"Of course," Dad said quickly. "Women seem to have their secrets all the time. I don't know how many times I've come into a room and she's been talking quietly with Lois or Carol and they stop talking immediately. A few times I asked what they were talking about but rarely got a straight answer."

"And didn't that bother you?" I asked.

"Yes and no," he replied. "I decided that if I needed to know she would tell me in her own time. Call it trust, or me not really caring, I don't really know which, but I decided it's easier than chewing myself up inside."

After a thoughtful pause he asked me, "Do you know about the aboriginal customs? They make it pretty clear."

I hadn't a clue what he was talking about so he explained.

"Generally women are not allowed to attend corroborees," he began. "Those are men's business. And there are sites that are designated as areas for secret women's business. Men wouldn't dare go there. Years ago a lot of black women were raped by whites and somehow the women got together and got rid of the foetuses. They had some way of giving abortions. But that was secret women's business. That society clearly delineated between men's business, at corroborees for instance, and women's business. And we have no idea really just what that may have involved overall."

Dad smiled. "To be honest, it's not a lot different with us, although the lines are not so clear. Traditionally men meet at the pub or the footy club, or go fishing or shooting together, and the women meet in their gossip sessions, sewing circles and such. But there are nowadays a lot more women in pubs and things where it might have been men only in the past. And maybe that's the problem."

I must have looked puzzled, as Dad explained just what he meant by that.

"In days gone by, men could meet as men, to share their interests and secrets. And women did the same. But in the current days of equality in most things, men and women are more inclined to do things together. And, when they don't, like when one seems to have a secret from the other, the problems start."

"So you don't think that men and women being together more and sharing everything is a good thing?" I asked.

"That's not what I said," my Dad replied. "I think it's a great thing - but it might explain why the being secretive bit is more of a problem now, when it probably wasn't so much of an issue previously."

"Can you tell me a little of what your big secret was about?" I asked, wondering if he would share it now.

He explained that he had a friend who was married but had started seeing another woman, who was also married. Dad didn't know how close their relationship was, but he knew they saw a lot of each other for a few months. Dad happened to see them together one day, parked down by the river.

When he had asked, the guy admitted it and asked Dad to keep it a secret. Dad agreed to, and he did. And he didn't say anything to my Mum because she knew both the woman involved and Dad's friend's wife. But really the secret didn't concern anyone else, provided it stayed a secret, and after a few months it was all over anyhow and no-one was the wiser.

"Don't you think, in some way anyway, that what they were doing was somehow, well, wrong? And that you knowing and keeping it secret might have made them think that what they were doing was alright?" I wasn't sure if my question was clear, but Dad knew what I meant.

He nodded. "That's where the judgement comes into it," he said. "I tried to weigh up what might be the consequences of me revealing their secret, for them, the two families, their children. For everyone really. Whether or not I agreed with what was going on didn't really come into it. I didn't agree with it, of course. But the hurt I might cause by telling others was my biggest concern. I decided that if they eventually wanted to cause suffering to others, that was their issue, but I didn't want to be the cause when it might never happen. So I kept their secret. That was my judgement at the time."

*

I called Mandy later that night and apologised for continuing to ask about her secret. The weather forecast was for another hot day so we arranged to meet the next morning.

We met at the corner and walked together through the streets and towards the river. Once at the river's edge we walked hand and hand along the bank until we arrived at Oddie's Creek Park and the grassy picnic area. There were a few family groups in the picnic area so we moved to one side of the park, to get a little privacy.

"So Tom," Mandy said once we were sitting on the grass in a quiet spot, "Have you changed your mind about needing to know my secret?"

She had a twinkle in her eyes and I felt she was teasing me.

"Not really, Mandy," I said, hugging her. "I would love to know it, but not enough to start an argument with you. I believe in you when you say it has nothing to do with me, or us. And I trust you and your judgement. Our friendship is more important to me Mandy, more important than some secret that probably doesn't matter anyway."

"Oh!" Mandy said, looking genuinely shocked. "And I'd made up my mind to tell you, and for the same reason. Because our friendship is more important."

"Dear Mandy," I said. "If you're convinced it has nothing to do with us and won't affect us, either of us, no matter what happens, I don't need to know it."

 I hugged her shoulders again. "If we trust and respect each other we must accept that we have the right to have secrets at times."

"But... but..." Mandy tried to say something. I just smiled and kissed her.

.o0o.

MONTY

By MAGGIE WILDBLOOD

Like most good writers, Maggie Wildblood is a keen observer of life. It's said that 'every person has a story', but if you don't know the person the opportunity is there for the imagination to go to work.

'Monty' is based on a chance encounter with a man who was interesting enough to inspire contemplation. Some people try not to look at the less fortunate in the community, perhaps thinking if they're ignored they'll just somehow go away. Maggie on the other hand looks deeper – how does that person feel, and think?

Monty can't put it off any longer. He's gotta get up, get out of bed. He pulls on baggy track pants, opens the door while dragging a t-shirt over his singlet, stumbles along the passage. Isn't hard to find, that lavatory, even in the dark. He just follows his nose. Few of the others, all of them men, give a toss about aiming; it's a hit or miss job for 'em. Most of 'em miss.

Back in his room, Monty knows there's no point getting under the blankets again. The warmth from his body has well and truly gone. Limping to the window, he pushes the grimy curtain aside. Rain. Rain, and wind as well. Typical bloody winter! Gets harder and harder every year. Impossible yet again to sit in the park and soak up some sun, warm his arthritic knees. Won't be tables and chairs on the footpath outside any of the cafes where a bloke could sit, linger over a coffee, watch the world pass him by.

Turning, he looks around. After ten years the room is as familiar to him as his own face: sagging bed shoved against the wall, bedding as grey as the weather; chair leaning drunkenly to one side; small table with a TV that works when it feels like it; elderly wardrobe with one door open, inside it a couple of coat hangers, wire bent in a V; a pair of runners, laces long gone and never replaced - why bother? - lying on the floor where he kicked them off last night. Not much to show for seventy-six years.

Old George in the room next door must be awake too. He coughs, and coughs again: a wet noise followed by a hawking sound before he spits into an old jar on the floor beside his bed. Smoker's cough, they called it once, but now it's got a fancy name, em-something. Or mebbe it's cancer. The result's the same, whatever you call it. He and George have shared that wall for a long time. Not many secrets between them, one way and another.

Suddenly Monty has to get out, be near other people, ordinary people. The weather affects him more than he likes to admit, takes him places he doesn't want to go to, wakens memories better left asleep. Days like this are the worst. They bring back the misery of school, the place he was ridiculed and punished by the teachers for his facial tics, for the noises and the words that sometimes burst from his mouth no matter how hard he tried to keep them in.

The playgrounds weren't playgrounds for Monty: they were places of torment and sometimes of torture. At last he'd found a hiding place under the main school building. There he'd crouch in the dark, the dirt and the spider's webs, when the other kids were out in the playground. Safe there he thought, until that wet winter's day when the big kids, all boys, found him.

They grabbed him, dragged him to the

toilet block. There they pulled down his pants, shoved his y-fronts into his mouth, pushed his head into the lavatory bowl and, pulled the chain. It was a big joke they thought, funny they thought, telling him to bark now, grunt now. The bell ringing for the end of 'playtime' saved him, forced the others back inside. Mr Osborne, the teacher, didn't even notice Monty wasn't there with the rest of the class. He'd nicked off home where his old man gave him a belting for getting wet.

 Mum and Dad weren't no help anyway, too busy getting pissed and abusing each other to spend any time worrying about their son the freak, Monty the monster. When he was reported for truancy, what did they do? They turned their abuse on him. Never bloody asked a kid why he nicked off, did they?

 It hadn't helped, finding out that these

almost uncontrollable spasms were something he'd been born with. Knowing a name, Tourette's Syndrome, doesn't matter, not any more anyway. Maybe it would've when he was a little tyke, but now? Hah!

Memorics: he tries to keep them buried in the dark, pushed down deep. Some kinds of dark are OK though, make him feel safe for a short while like he did under the school building. That's it, that's what he'll do. Go to the movies, burrow into the dark of the Dendy for a couple of hours.

Sliding his feet into the runners and shrugging on his jacket, a trophy from Vinnies, he grabs his stick, hobbles to the door.

Catching a glimpse of himself in the wardrobe mirror he sees a no. 2 cut; a face that's subsided into wrinkled despair; track pants and top; jacket and stick; and the runners. Now that's a laugh: it's been years since he's run anywhere. The idea of it almost makes him smile. Better take the old Ansett airline bag as well, might do a bit of shopping.

The wind grabs the front door and slams it shut before he can. It's much colder out here on the street. He'd thought his room was cold but there was no wind there, well, apart from the bloody draught that whines through the gaps around the window frame. Here on the street there's wind all right, wind that whips spikes of rain around a man's legs, down his collar.

What's on at the Dendy? Oh hell, it doesn't matter. A bloke just wants to sit in the warm dark, out of reach of the rain and the wind. And away from the eyes watching him as he tics and twitches, away from the ears that hear his words and sounds, away from the looks of pity, distaste, condemnation. It's the pity that's the worst, but, nibbles away at the little bit of pride still deep inside him. That pride – it's all a bloke's got left.

 He passes the pub, then doubles back, popping in for a quickie, a winter warmer. After downing a rum, then another, he goes into the bottle shop and gets a longie and a half bottle of rum. Just what the doctor ordered, as the old man used to say. Into the Ansett bag they slide, separated by the newspaper he keeps there to stop the bottles clinking or worst of all, breaking. After paying for the grog there isn't much left, but enough for the movie. He's made sure of that. Pension day's coming up, and it won't be the first time he's run short. Or the last.

 Out in the weather again, he struggles

across King Street near the traffic lights, impatient horns blasting at him. No walking on the pedestrian crossing for him.

He looks at the drivers sitting in their air-conditioned comfort, gives them the finger, shuffles past the shops and plunges into the Dendy's foyer. The aroma of hot food from the cafe taunts him. He'd give quids to be able to buy a hot drink, maybe even a pie.

Then he laughs at himself, muttering under his breath, "You pays your money and you takes your choice and mine was grog."

The young bloke behind the counter has smooth hair and smooth skin, looks about sixteen. He raises an eyebrow at Monty.

"Yeah?"

"Pensioner's ticket, mate."

"Whad'a ya wanta see?"

"Whatever's on soonest, mate."

"OK, here's a ticket to *The Journey of the Red Balloon*. It's a French film, starts in ten in Cinema Two."

In the theatre he picks a seat in the back row near the door. The place is almost empty, just a few old birds sitting in singles. They'd have looked like chooks on a roost except from what he remembers, chooks huddle together and this lot don't, no, not them. They're more like birds on a wire. No one takes any notice as he manoeuvres himself down, leaning his stick against the seat to the left, settling the airline bag on his lap, quietly undoing its zipper. There it is, his little friend, shedding drops of condensation onto the brown paper bag that the bloke in the bottle shop insisted on using. His fingers find his other friend, nestling beside the longie, ready when he is.

As soon as the theatre's dark, he slides the bag down the longie's neck. Pushing his thumbs under its corrugations, he lifts the lid off, places it carefully, noiselessly, back in the bag. The comforting smell of hops fills his nostrils. On the screen, ads rush past and the movie begins. He saw *The Red Balloon* years ago. Will it have been changed much? Probably. Everything seems to be changing these days, and fast. Even he's changing, but not for the better.

Relaxing now, he raises the bottle to his lips, rewarded by the wetness sliding down his throat.

By God, that's good. Better take it easy though, better take it easy. No need to rush things. Movies usually last about an hour and a half, and if he's careful, takes his time, spaces it out, the grog should last that long. Knows himself too well to think there'll be anything left to take 'home'.

A bark, his bark, echoes in the theatre. A voice, his voice, says, loud-like, 'Thanks very much."

He lifts the bottle again. And again. Over and over. He's surprised when, suddenly it seems, it's empty.

From his mouth, again: "Ugh." Then, "Number one."

It's started. It usually starts when he relaxes, especially with a few on board. There are times when he can control the words, even though it's so bloody hard it's almost not worth the effort.

But sometimes it just gets too much for

him and he has to let go, let the noises and the words fall out.

Better have a rum now the bloody beer's gone. Frigging screw tops are hard enough in the light, let alone in the dark. Determined, he struggles and succeeds. Worth the effort. Definitely. The rum burns and warms as it goes down, a terrific contrast to the beer. The more it burns and warms, the less he cares. As the liquor flows, so do his words, his sounds.

He can feel the muscles under his eye, down the left side of his face, ticcing, but no one can see them. The sounds are different, they're loud, getting louder. He senses the restlessness around him. A woman turns, hisses, "Shhhh."

"I would if I could, lady," he wants to tell her, shout out to the whole bloody theatre. "When you've got Tourette's, you don't have a say in what you say."

 Long ago he learned there's no point, no point at all, in trying to explain. No one really understands TS. No one gives a shit anyway. He's just another old bloke stumbling around, another weirdo.

 He opens his mouth, lifts the bottle to take a swig. Before he can drink he's afloat in a river of sounds: 'fuck' and 'shit', and then 'thank you' and then 'ugly bitch' and then 'number one.' Then some grunts, a couple of barks. Come on Monty, come on, stop stuffing around! Get that rum into ya! Keep the mouth busy, fill it with something else! But the words, the sounds, they're like water pouring out. At last he manages to stop the flow with the neck of the bottle, takes a swig, clamps his mouth shut as he swallows.

 He doesn't notice the woman, the one

who shushed him, getting up and going outside.

"Sir, I'll have to ask you to leave."

 A man's quiet voice beside him.

'The movie, I've paid to see the bloody movie!" Monty waves the bottle at the screen.

"Yes I know sir, but you have to leave. *Now*!"

"But..."

"Look, sir – we'll give you your money back!"

 In the darkness, Monty finds the lid of the rum, carefully screws it back on, puts the precious bottle back in the bag, and fumbles for his stick. Just as well there's all that space between the rows. Lurching towards the open door, he shivers as cold streams in with the light from the foyer. He's escaped the loneliness, the humiliation, for almost an hour. Back to reality now.

 The movie's a dead loss, what he's seen of it, anyway. They stuffed it up good and proper. The first one, the one he remembers from forty years ago, was better. Much better, just like a bloke was, forty years ago.

 Then he remembers something else. Grinning, he pats his bag, feels the comforting outline of the rum bottle.

 There *is* a little something to take home after all.

.o0o.

GAME GIRL

By MEREDITH YARDLEY

Through her business 'Happiness-Worx', Meredith pursues a mission to improve the lives of as many people as possible in her community. She operates Laughter Clubs and a regular Jigsaw Club, all helping people to overcome one of the great scourges of our society: loneliness.

Not all kids turn to games out of loneliness, but many do. Games are a place to escape to. To find or make friends, real or imaginary. A safe place, where you might actually feel like you're in control. That's the theory, anyway.

'Tina, come to dinner.'

'Tina, clean up your room.'

'Tina, time for school.'

'Tina. Tina! Shut down that game and get ready for bed!'

Tina didn't hear her Mum. She was too busy playing 'Thwart', the new game she had been give for her fifteenth birthday. It was a mystery gift, arriving in the post without a card, but very much addressed to her: Mistress Tina Nolan. None of her grandparents would admit to sending it. None of her uncles or aunts would have spent that sort of money on a game for her, not when they had their own children to buy for.

A mystery gift. She liked the thought of that. No-one else she knew had received a mystery gift. She took her laptop to school and played it during lunchtime and recess, and instead of being bullied like she often was, the Coterie, a bunch of bitchy girls who travelled in a pack and made her life miserable, were now jealous of the attention she was getting from The Bulls (another gang, but these were boys).

But at least it meant that the Coterie left her alone.

The Bulls all had Dungeons and Dragons, Counterstrike and Diablo, but no-one had heard of 'Thwart' before. And it was a really wicked game - with great graphics and fantastic sounds that made it look like people's heads were blown up, and with car bombs just like on the nightly television news. When she used to watch it. Now she just played Thwart.

All the time.

It took a while to understand the rules. The game didn't have any written down anywhere that she could find, so she just learned by trial and error. She got blown away a lot of times, sometimes she drowned, sometimes she was assassinated, sometimes she was tortured. But she was a quick learner, and it wasn't long before she left behind the beginner's level of Private and became a Corporal. She wasn't sure how far the levels went, maybe even to General! So that left a long way to go.

But sometimes, just sometimes, she felt like she wasn't in her room when she was playing. Sometimes, she felt the game was surrounding her, like she was *in* it. Maybe that was what was meant by 'focus' that they had talked about at school - that you really, truly got inside something you liked.

Now The Bulls kept ringing her at home, wanting to come over and play Thwart at her house, or inviting her to their places. But the more they pestered her, the more she kept it for herself.

Mum had said how nice it was she was making friends at the new school. It was hard, all this moving around because of Dad's job in the Army, but hopefully, she had said, this job would be for a while and they could settle down and things would be different.

She tried to make friends. Tina hated to see that little furrow of worry between her Mum's eyebrows. She knew her Mum worried about her a lot, she was always asking lots of questions - in a nice, round about way, so that maybe Tina wouldn't realise she was quizzing her. But she knew what Mum was doing.

To please her, she tried sports, ball sports at first, netball, cricket, tennis. But she was hopelessly uncoordinated and was always the last kid picked for a team.

Sometimes teams would even prefer to play one person short than have her on the side.

Then she tried swimming. That was a disaster too - she nearly drowned because one of The Coterie had thought it was funny to hold her by her legs under water in the deep end so she couldn't get up for air. That had really frightened her.

Athletics? Forget it - way too lanky and gangly, with legs splaying out and arms windmilling as she ran.

The chess club held no charms for her at all - she was too good, she never lost, so no-one wanted to play against her any more. Even the nerds didn't want her.

So whoever had sent her Thwart did her a huge favour. Because she played it at school, and the other kids wanted to play

it too, when it hit the market, the sales from the town went through the roof. The local shop had had to place three orders in the first ten days. Mr Isaac, the shop's owner, told Mum at the local Rotary meeting, that that had never ever happened before in the history of gaming. It was even bigger than a new Apple release. For their small town anyway.

Over the year, she got through all the levels. She became a General! She was both elated and devastated by this. Elated because she had mastered the game - she was right, General was as far as you could go. All the kids at school were still trying to get past the beginner levels, but she finished the game. Now what would she do?

The Bulls kept asking her for tips on how to play, but that wasn't how the game worked. You *had* to figure it out for yourself or you were punished. Somehow the game knew if someone got coached - and something ended up happening beyond the player's control, and they got busted down a rank.

So she was pretty glum on her sixteenth birthday. She wandered in the back door after school and bam! She saw it. Right there in the middle of the kitchen table was a parcel addressed to General Tina Nolan.

'How odd,' Mum said. 'It could almost be for your father, but, well, everything is wrong about that address. Well,' her brow furrowed, and Tina thought for a moment she wouldn't let her have it, 'well, it *is* addressed to you, in a weird way. I suppose you'd better open it.'

Tina could feel the excitement bubbling inside her. It was a new game, she was sure of it! She took the parcel, which was much smaller than the one Thwart had been, and started to walk to her room.

'No Tina,' Mum said. 'I want to see what it is. Please open it here'.

She could hardly refuse. She put the parcel on the kitchen table. She undid the sticky tape, all very carefully. Mum took the brown paper and spread it out flat on the table, peering at the stamps. Then she got a magnifying glass to see them even more clearly, but they didn't seem to tell her anything.

Tina heard her on the phone soon after speaking to Dad who was away on a three month secondment interstate. 'I tell you, Steve, it's weird. No card, the return address is actually our address, the stamps are nothing special, and the postmark is too smudged for me to make out where it was sent from.'

There was silence while Dad must have been talking.

'No, it seems to be just another computer game. I've looked it up on the internet and I couldn't find it. And so I looked up the first one she got, that Thwart thing she just couldn't stop playing - and it wasn't released onto the market until three months after she received hers in the post. And Mike Isaacs, yeah, the guy who owns the tech store in town, said he'd never seen anything like it the way that game sold out. It's just weird.'

 Silence again.

'Well, it seems the girls have stopped teasing her, and boys are becoming more friendly, although she doesn't seem very enthusiastic. She gets lots of phone calls asking if she can go visit them at their homes, but she just stays home and plays Thwart. Now here's another game and I have a feeling it's just going to get worse. I really wish you were home.'

Silence while Dad spoke.

'I know, I know, I just worry about her, that's all. I know you do too love, I'm looking forward to you coming home. No, I can't remember the name of the new game. No, it's not Thwart 2, but I'll look it up and see what I can find out and let you know when you can call next. Yes, love you too...'

So Tina was safe. Dad hadn't said Mum should take the new game away, which is what she was worried about.

She took the purple USB and slid it into the computer. A whirring sound started, then it became a chugging sound, then a small blast, a puff of smoke, and the USB was almost spat from the machine.

The screen came to life, looking like a million tiny stars, which started to meld

and become silver. Then the silver slowly faded away and she was at what she
figured was the starting page. The screen
was green.

 She clicked on a pulsating blue button in
the middle of the screen, the only thing
on the screen, and began. First she was
prompted to choose a name for herself,
not from a list. She had to make it up. She
chose Rovik because it wasn't obviously
male or female.

 She then entered a new password, using a
number of different codes chosen from all
over the screen.   She created her avatar -
a vertical green ribbon. That should be a
good camouflage, and would give her the
ability to, not fly exactly, but float through
the air. Because she had a feeling that
camouflage and the ability to be airborne
would be important.

From the very beginning, this game was totally different to Thwart. Even its name was super weird.

She reckoned it would take a while to get the hang of it. As well as creatures and animals that looked familiar, there were animals she'd never seen before, such as three legged scaly creatures, with long tails; fat creatures with stumpy legs that looked like rhinos, but had horns all over their bodies; creatures with wings - some looked like birds with feathers and some looked like flying cats, with fur and tails; and something like a stingray that flew. It was brilliantly silent. There were also machines; tall ones with long leg-like things that stepped over trees; short stumpy ones that could walk through rocks - well not through them, but walk into boulders and the boulders would disintegrate.

There were people too - sort of. They

stood upright, and most had two legs, although some had one and others three. The same with arms, although it seemed that the more arms they had the fewer legs they had, and the other way around. Some could fly, without wings or any sort of external propulsion that she could see; others could only stay on the ground, but they didn't seem to walk, more glide.

But most of all, including the great graphics, it had *smells*! She'd never even heard of a game that had smells! Rich earthy smells in the forest; sweet smells that wafted out into her room for some animals; rank, sick smells for other creatures.

The first level was pretty basic. She had to turn some of the weird creatures into something totally different; and they seemed to have some sort of power to stop her. She got zapped a couple of times, and it actually *hurt*! And when she looked, there was definitely a red mark on her ankle, and one on her left shoulder.

But she managed to survive - some of the other players weren't so lucky. And that was what was also weird about this game, because she wasn't hooked up to the internet, but she wasn't the only one playing.

There was someone called Greeve, who had an eyepatch, and another player, Swallow, who had long, flowing blond hair; Riloria who travelled in a suit and tie (how weird was that!) and Maizaro, who just glimmered - becoming stronger when they had won a challenge. She knew they were other players because they sent her messages in real time.

As she played, her fingers flew over the keyboard giving orders, making demands, typing in codes she was making up as she went along.

'Tina, time for bed.'

'Bed!' one of the gliding human things
chortled 'the Army brat has to go to bed
- don't you touch her' it blasted a flying
stingray, 'she's mine and I'm going to
absorb her.' And the thing glided straight
at her! She slammed the laptop lid shut.
Just for a moment she thought he saw a
lump under the lid. But she shook her
head, and then wasn't so sure.

So she went to bed. To think. What was
this Xnggox game, she wondered as she
fell asleep.

*

Tina liked weekends. She was pretty free
to do what she liked as long as she could
prove to Mum she'd done her homework

by Saturday lunchtime. Now that the ridiculous focus on sports had passed, she could just hang out on the computer. Mum was cool, said she was old enough now to look after herself during the day. So Mum was able to catch up with friends for lunch, go to the gym, all the things she liked to do. And she wanted Mum to do these things - Mum was lonely when Dad was away and Tina liked it when Mum came home happy.

Tina waved goodbye to her after she had promised she'd make a sandwich AND clean up afterwards. She locked the front and back doors, and sat down at her desk.

She ran her hand over the top of the laptop. There was no damage to the lid - she must have imagined that lump. She carefully opened it. The screen was black. She pressed the ON button, entered her password, and clicked on the Xnggox icon to start the game.

 The screen opened to a view of a forest she'd never seen before. The tree trunks were normal coloured, the leaves were blue, or green, or purple and strange shapes - triangles, circles, squares. Who had ever heard of square leaves, for goodness sake! Maybe this really was a kiddy game after all.   But it smelled like compost - so she figured it was probably a friendly forest.

 Then the sound started. A slow buzzing sound, she couldn't see anything, but it got gradually louder and louder. She was prepared for anything, she thought. She had her Disc - a powerful implement shaped like a discus, behaved like a boo-merang with the power of a wand, you threw it and it returned to you after doing its duty which could be knocking a crea-ture unconscious to escape, or zapping an enemy so they were paralysed and you could steal their weaponry; or aiming truly at what passed for their heart-space and killing them. They all had a heart-space in a different place, so killing one didn't happen very often - but she was getting better.

She had a good position at the mouth of a shallow cave so nothing could come up behind her. She had already nominated several woodland creatures to do her bidding - and the rules of the game seemed to be that they had no choice, so she was as ready as he could be with her own small army.

At first she had thought you needed tigers and lions and bears - big, strong, aggressive animals to do your bidding.

Then she realised that actually the small, fluffy creatures such as rabbits, possums, squirrels, martens and birds were better.

Birds were really good because of their speed. Snakes were great, but sometimes a bit slow depending on whether they were warm enough - but a quick moving snake would get rid of a yellow horned creature faster than just about anything. And if you set a ferret onto a short machine, well the sparks would fly but the ferret would win two out of three times, maybe because the machine expected something like a rhino or polar bear he could barge through and destroy and was taken by surprise.

So the buzzing was a new thing - and she figured she must have advanced another level. And then she saw it. A swarm of bees. Damn, she hadn't thought of them - one of her enemies, or even another player - had got them first. This was going to be tough - quick thinking was needed.

She climbed up the nearest tree and plastered as many leaves over herself as she could - and it wasn't long before she was completely covered. The swarm was circling, and the circles were getting smaller - spiralling from the sky towards her. She grabbed the bee hive just above her head and turned it upside down on herself, with the honey running all over the leaves. Within seconds the bees had landed on her - and stuck to the honey. When the buzzing had stopped, she thought of the birds - and it had to be sea birds such as oyster catchers, and herons, with long beaks - and they came. They carefully removed each and every leaf with the bees stuck to it and she was freed.

Tina moved the hive into the tree, and left it near all the leaves the birds had removed. By vanquishing the bees she had the choice for them to be part of her arsenal. So she chanted and zap - they became part of her army.

 There were other challenges Tina faced
- and she advanced up the levels every
time. Her strategy of claiming the smaller,
seemingly weaker creatures seemed to be
paying off.

 Other players weren't so lucky. Greeve
lost his life against the giant machines -
he had thought that armouring himself
mostly with ridgeback canines was going
to work. It so didn't, they just weren't
a match for the scaly creatures the machines set on him.

 Riloria was a surprise - she kept her
gender hidden really well and that had
worked well, as her enemies launched
attacks that were made for males. Very
smart. But she made one fatal mistake,
she forgot to pee standing up - and then it
was only a matter of time before the

mistrals got her.

Maizaro was different. Tina still wasn't
sure how the glimmering worked - she
hadn't been able to figure out how to do
something like that. It was so successful
Maizaro was at a higher level, and no-one
else could lay claim to that. Tina wasn't
sure if Maizaro was male or female, or
whether Maizaro knew she existed or not,
but figured it must know about her if she
knew about it.

She had to think about what her next
strategy would be. Should she take the
risk and try to Connect with Maizaro? Or
would that mean certain death? If they
could be united, their strength could win
them the game. But could Maizaro be
trusted?

She retreated into 'The Sanctuary' to
think. She had built it herself. She wasn't

able to stay there long, but it did give her time to reflect in safety. The rules of the game wouldn't allow her to retreat while hostilities were occurring, it was only allowed in 'The Gentle' - the time when the enemy nursed their wounds, or regrouped. You really had to be on your toes to know when The Gentle was, to make the most of the time. The blue triangle was the clue. If you missed the blue triangle - which was *really* easy to do because it just kind of flickered in a different place on the screen each time, you lost the chance to take a breather.

So she cleaved to her Sanctuary. And thought.

She looked at the game from all the different perspectives she could imagine that would help her win: garnering more animals; trying to override an enemy war-machine and then using it against other enemy troops; identifying and laying claim to a series of hiding spaces and making them invisible - but they all had too many risks attached.

She made a decision that the risks of approaching Maizaro were not as great as the risks of them *not* Connecting. But she couldn't do it in her usual avatar. She would have to shed the disguise so hopefully Maizaro would recognise she wasn't to be feared. That's where the danger was. For while the chances were good that Maizaro would know she wasn't a threat, the enemy could find her really quickly - and her chance to get the Red Stone would be lost.

For they were all fighting to find, and then harness the power of, the Red Stone. She couldn't believe it had taken four levels to figure this out - but the Red Stone was the power in the Game. And all the enemy's forces would fight forever to discover it and take it from its hiding place deep in the forest. The Red Stone would allow whoever held it to rule the land.

And of course, how do you communicate to a Glimmer? She didn't have the power to glimmer - it was a high level skill, and she was more than a bit impressed by it.

She only had a short time left in the Sanctuary to work on her strategy. She couldn't Glimmer, but perhaps, just perhaps, she could figure out where Maizaro was most likely to be, build up her energy by relinquishing her ownership of the creatures, and use that power to Vibrate.

That was it! She would throw all of her power into the one, strong, long, Vibration.

So she waited until the quietest part of

the Arc (the Xnggox version of days, she hadn't figured out yet if there were weeks, months or even seasons), located herself in the area where she thought Maizaro would be, on The Boulder - a massive, single piece of stone that kept the hot water from the powerful Lilac Wood at bay - spun her disc through the air above her head, releasing ownership of the small creatures, and crooned to Maizaro, Vibrating.

'Tina, I'm home.'

Shit! Not now.

'Tina, where are you honey? I've bought you a new t-shirt, I think you'll really like it.'

Vibrate. Just focus on Vibrating. Maizaro - join with me - let us own the Red Stone together. You and I can own ....

'Tina?'

She looked up. Her mother was peering at her through what looked like a dirty lens.

'Tina, that looks like you.' Mum shook her head, 'But that's ridiculous. You can't be *in* the game. Where are you?' Mum looked around the room. 'Are you using a camera or something...? Tina, answer me!'

'Mum, Mum, it's okay, I'm okay,' she tried to say, but she just Vibrated.

'Tina? Where are you?' The voice getting further away, 'Where are you?'

Tina felt a warmth behind her, then around her arms and legs. The Glimmering was wrapping itself around her, and as she Vibrated into it, her mother's voice was getting further and further away; her bedroom getting darker and darker until it wasn't there any more.

And then it was just her Vibrating into the Glimmering until... until the Glimmering started to fade and her Vibration got stronger. Tina Vibrated so strongly that she could actually *see* the air move in waves around her. But not see with her eyes, more like see with her *being*. There was a sweet smell in the air, kind of like the perfume Mum wore when she and Dad went out on one of their 'dates'.

She didn't know what that meant. In fact, it was starting to get a little frightening and she wanted to stop. But she couldn't, her Vibration just kept getting louder and louder and the creatures that had silently followed her to capture her, started to back away. Some tripped and scurried away on the ground, some just turned and got as far away as possible - turning into little dots in the distance, and where her head should be got higher and higher and she felt bigger and bigger and then...

'Bloody game!' said Mum, walking back into Tina's bedroom. She walked over to the laptop and slammed the lid down.

.oOo.

ABOUT THE OLD BASTARDS

There was this war, see? There'd already been The War To End All Wars, but then another one came along, so they called it World War 2.

In the course of this bloody great unpleasantness a bunch of American service- men got posted to Australia. It didn't always work out well – I'm not going to talk about the Battle Of Brisbane - but there was good stuff came out of the whole mess.

One or two of those visitors were particularly struck by the fact that in Australia "G'day ya old bastard!" was an expression of mateship, not the precursor to a fight. When they got back 'stateside' they kicked off something called the Inter- national Order Of Old Bastards.

Fast forward twenty or so years to 1968. In the British Lion Hotel, Glebe, a bloke named Leo Bradshaw and some mates decided to reclaim the term and kick off the Australasian Order Of Old Bastards. (At least one of the regulars was a Kiwi.) Leo and his mates were determined to raise as much money as possible for Camperdown's Royal Alexandra Hospital For Children, and the AOOB was to be their way of doing it.

The name caused a few problems. It was (and still is) a bit hard to convince some people to take seriously a charitable organization that so clearly doesn't take itself too seriously. But they stuck to their guns, and in 1973 the AOOB was officially recognized and registered as a charity. (It's now A.C.N. 11032, if you want to be precise.)

New branches and new charities have come along. Camperdown Children's is now Westmead, but is still important to the AOOB. At last count the hospital had received over $1.5 million from the Old Bastards. All up, as of August 2019 over seven and a half million dollars has been raised and donated. Not bad, eh?

Life membership of the AOOB will only cost you $15, and you can sign up on the website: www.aoob.com.au - tell 'em I nominated you (#334752).

This book has been organized by the Northern Rivers branch of the AOOB as a part of WordFest 2019, with the proud support of the publishers *Meredian Pictures and Words.* All of the profits from sales will be being directed by the AOOB to Story Dogs Inc.

Story Dogs is a really clever initiative that takes dogs (and their owners) into schools to help kids who've got literacy problems. The kid reads to the dog – a completely happy, non-critical audience – and gradually learns to actually *enjoy* reading. It becomes fun, not a chore, and when that happens it often becomes easier. That's the way with things we enjoy doing, eh? You *want* to practice, and the more you do the better you get at it.

The NSW Northern Rivers is an interesting place. People here seem to think a bit differently to those in many other parts of the country. I won't say "think *more*" but I do reckon a lot people here are good at being what's now called 'mindful'.

It's probably no coincidence that the region has more yoga teachers per head of population than anywhere else in Australia.

It's that mindfulness that led to the anthology's title - folks' minds do run deep.

A big round of thanks to the authors who've contributed the stories you've just read. Bette, Karl, Steve, Ray, Maggie and Meredith - as generous as they are creative. None of them are getting any royalties. So as well as their talent, they share a commitment to encouraging people to read.

I hope you've enjoyed this collection, and I hope that enjoyment is added to by knowing you've done somebody some good by buying it. (Of course, if you *didn't* buy it and you pinched it from someone, you better figure that karma is an Old Bastard too, and keep looking over your shoulder...) Thanks for reading.

Cheers!

Henri Rennie

Secretary -*Australasian Order of Old Bastards*
Northern Rivers Branch